triangle

circle

oval

crescent

square

heart

rectangle

semicircle

Story based on the characters from Max Lucado's *Hermie: A Common Caterpillar.*
Visit us at: www.hermieandfriends.com
Email us at: comments@hermieandfriends.com

Illustrations by GlueWorks Animation.

Published in Nashville, Tennessee, by Tommy Nelson®, a Division of Thomas Nelson, Inc.

The publisher thanks June Ford, Amy Parker, Troy Schmidt, Holly Gusick, and Kathleen Vaghy for their assistance in the preparation of this book.

Library of Congress Cataloging-in-Publication Data

Lucado, Max.
 Shapes [illustration by GlueWorks Animation].
    p. cm. — (Buginnings)
 "Based on the characters from Max Lucado's Hermie: a common caterpillar."
 ISBN 1-4003-0421-0 (hardback)
 1. Shapes—Juvenile literature. I. GlueWorks Animation. II. Title. III. Series.
 QA445.5.N45 2004
 516'.15—dc22   2004000465

Printed in the United States of America
04 05 06 07 08 PHX 5 4 3 2 1

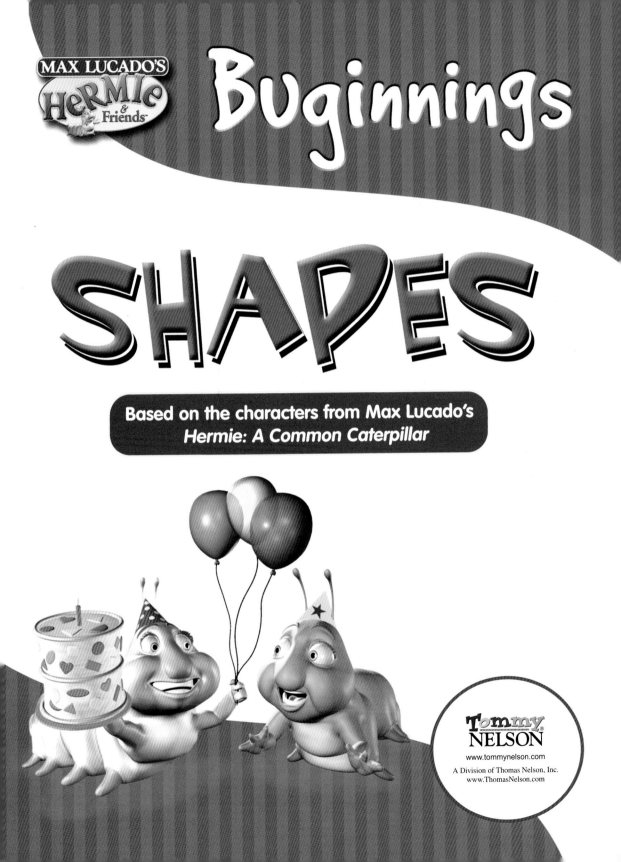

MAX LUCADO'S
HERMIE
&
Friends

Buginnings

SHAPES

Based on the characters from Max Lucado's
Hermie: A Common Caterpillar

Tommy
NELSON®
www.tommynelson.com
A Division of Thomas Nelson, Inc.
www.ThomasNelson.com

Wormie the caterpillar was having a birthday party for Hermie. And all their garden friends had come.

"Let's play Guess the Shape!" Wormie said. He knew it was Hermie's favorite game.

"Me first!" Hermie said.

"Guess, guess. Guess if you can. I'm round like the sun. What shape did I make?" Hermie asked.

"Circle, circle. You made a circle," Wormie shouted.

Now it was Wormie's turn to make a shape. He asked Hermie to help him.

circle

"Guess, guess. Guess if you can. We're longer than a circle. What shape did we make?" Wormie asked.

"**Oval**, oval. You made an oval," Antonio Ant said.

Now it was Antonio's turn to make a shape. And he chose Annie Ant and Captain Ant to help him.

oval

"Guess, guess. Guess if you can. We are the shape of a mountaintop. What shape did we make?" asked Antonio, Annie, and Captain Ant.

"Triangle, triangle. You made a triangle," the Ladybug twins said with a giggle.

Now it was the twins' turn to make a shape.

triangle

"Mama, Mama," said Hailey and Bailey Ladybug as they flew forward with their wings spread wide.

"Guess, guess. Guess if you can. We are the shape of strawberries. What shape did we make?" asked Hailey and Bailey.

"**Hearts**, hearts. You made twin polka-dotted hearts," Lucy Ladybug said proudly.

Now it was Lucy's turn to make a shape.

heart

Lucy rolled to her back and tucked in her arms and legs.

"Guess, guess. Guess if you can. It's the shape of a smile. What shape did I make?" Lucy asked.

"Semicircle, semicircle. You made a semicircle," Puffy the dragonfly said with a great big smile.

Now it was Puffy's turn to make a shape.

semicircle

"Guess, guess. Guess if you can. It's the shape of a banana. What shape did I make?" Puffy asked.

"Crescent, crescent. You made a crescent," Caitlin Caterpillar said.

Now it was Caitlin's turn to make a shape, and she asked Hermie, Wormie, and Milt to help her.

crescent

"Guess, guess. Guess if you can. It's the shape of a box. What shape did we make?" asked Hermie, Wormie, Milt, and Caitlin.

"**Square**, square. You made a square," Schneider Snail said.

Now it was Schneider's turn to make a shape. But he needed some help, too.

square

"Guess, guess. Guess if you can. Together, we made a shape like a square, but longer. What shape did we make?" Schneider Snail asked.

"That's easy!" everyone shouted. "**Rectangle**, rectangle. We made a rectangle!"

And now it was time for birthday cake. And Wormie had a surprise for Hermie!

rectangle

"A shapes clown! Wormie, this is my best birthday ever, thanks to you!" Hermie said.

After all the cake was eaten and the presents were opened . . .

Guess, guess. Guess if you can. What game did they play?

"Let's play Guess the Shape! again," Hermie said. "And this time, let's see how fast we can make the shapes!"

And they did!

circle

oval

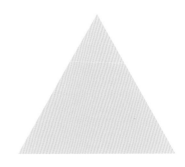

triangle

heart

semicircle

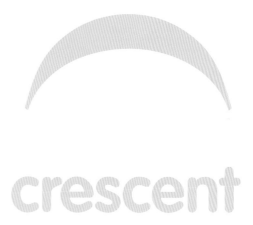

crescent

square

rectangle